At the Beach

Anne & Harlow Rockwell

MACMILLAN PUBLISHING COMPANY · NEW YORK

COLLIER MACMILLAN PUBLISHERS · LONDON

Copyright © 1987 by Anne Rockwell and Harlow Rockwell
All rights reserved. No part of this book may be reproduced
or transmitted in any form or by any means, electronic or
mechanical, including photocopying, recording or by any
information storage and retrieval system, without
permission in writing from the Publisher.
Macmillan Publishing Company
866 Third Avenue, New York, N.Y. 10022
Collier Macmillan Canada, Inc.
Printed and bound by
South China Printing Company,
Hong Kong
First American Edition
10 9 8 7 6 5 4 3 2 1
The text of this book is set in 24 point Spartan Book.
The illustrations are rendered in pencil and watercolor.
Library of Congress Cataloging-in-Publication Data
Rockwell, Anne F. At the beach.
Summary: A child experiences enjoyable sights and
sounds during a day at the beach.
1. Bathing beaches—Juvenile literature. 2. Outdoor
recreation—Juvenile literature. 3. Seashore—Juvenile
literature. [1. Seashore. 2. Beaches] I. Rockwell,
Harlow. II. Title.
GV191.62.R63 1987 910'.0914'6 86-2943
ISBN 0-02-777940-8

I wear my bathing suit
and I bring my shovel and pail
when I go to the beach.

We bring our towels
and beach umbrella
and tote bag with us.

In the tote bag
there are two cups
and a thermos of lemonade.

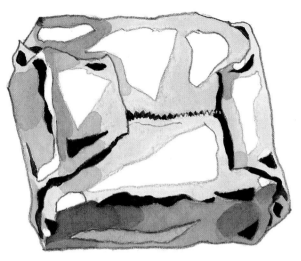
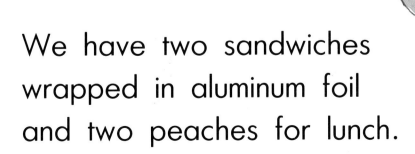

We have two sandwiches
wrapped in aluminum foil
and two peaches for lunch.

There is a tube of sunscreen
to rub on our skin
so we don't get sunburned.
I like the way
the sunscreen smells.

Little sandpipers run
down the beach
and I follow them.

My feet make footprints
in the wet sand.
The sandpipers make footprints, too.

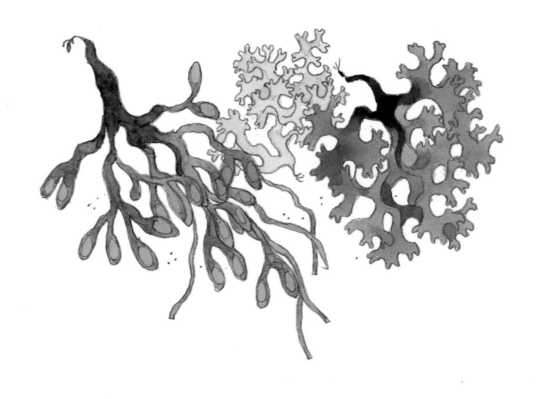

I find some seaweed

and seashells on the beach.

I build a castle with my shovel and pail.
The boy next to me digs a channel
where his boat can float.

Everyone is building something
in the sand at the beach.

I wade in the water.
A little crab tweaks my toe,
and little silver fishes
swim past me.

I like to walk
past the lifeguard's station
to the big, brown rocks.

That is where the barnacles
and snails and mussels live.

When my mother and I go swimming,
the waves crash on us
and get us all wet.
A big sea gull swims close to us.

Then I lie on my towel
and dry myself in the hot sun
until it is time

for lunch.